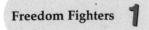

Midnight

**JENNY PAUSACKER**

Illustrated by Brian Harrison

A Haights Cross Communications Company

Published by
Sundance Publishing
P.O. Box 740
One Beeman Road
Northborough, MA 01532
800-343-8204

Copyright © text Jenny Pausacker 2001
Copyright © illustrations Brian Harrison 2001

First published 2001 as Supa Dazzlers by
Pearson Education Australia Pty Limited
95 Coventry Street
South Melbourne 3205 Australia
Exclusive United States Distribution: Sundance Publishing

ISBN 0-7608-6169-2

# Contents

# I Meet Jalen

My friend Jalen ended up as a famous hero. But when I first met him, he didn't look like a hero. He wasn't very tall or good-looking, like heroes are supposed to be. He was just very annoying!

I met Jalen on the planet called Earth, at Ms. Mack's Children's Home for Intelligent Life Forms. I'd ended up there when my parents' spaceship crashed in the ocean. A fishing boat found me swimming around a coral reef. I was trying to talk to some jellyfish.

I was the only Alph at the Home, so I felt pretty lonely. While the others were playing in the yard, I'd sneak off and go walking around the place.

I guess I was still searching for my mothers and fathers. I was just a kid then. I couldn't believe that my five parents were gone for good.

And that's when I first saw Jalen. Well, I really heard him first. A funny sound was coming from Ms. Mack's office. I pushed open the door. There he was, sitting in the seat by the window. Wet stuff was coming out of his eyes.

When I touched his cheek with my taste-tentacle, he gasped. Then he rubbed his hand across his face. He looked like he was ashamed of the wet stuff. I thought that was odd. I'd be really proud of myself if I could make water with my eye.

"Oh, great," he said, glaring at me. "Just what I need. A monster. What are you doing here, Blob? Have you come to frighten me? Or are you planning to eat me for lunch?"

He was talking in Standard Earthspeak. But I could understand him, of course. You see, Alphs have a layer in our brains that works like a translator unit. So I knew what *monster* meant. And I didn't like it, not one little bit! After all, Jalen looked weird himself. He had two arms, two legs, funny-looking fur on his head, and smooth, pale skin all over his body. He looked pretty strange and creepy, if you want my opinion.

"Listen to me. My name isn't Blob," I snapped. "It's Dizil. And by the way, I'm not a monster! I'm an Alph—from Alpha Centauri. And I think that you are very, very, *very* rude!"

Jalen shrugged. (That was his way of saying that he didn't care what I thought.) "So you're an Alph?" he said, frowning. Then he walked to the window and pointed outside. "What are *they*?" he asked.

I pressed my eye-tentacle against the glass. A gray lizard with rough skin was wrestling with a ball of electric sparks. Nearby, a bunch of strange-looking aliens watched and cheered them on.

"They're the other orphans," I explained. "Rasska, the tall gray one, comes from Repto. Fflit, the ball of sparks, comes from Mars. And the rest of them come from different places and planets all over the solar system."

"Yes, I can see that," Jalen said, clearly annoyed. "But I can't see any other humans. Am I the only kid from Earth?"

"Well," I said, "Ms. Mack says that Earthers are allowed only one kid each. And some people can't have kids at all. So leftover kids get adopted quickly. Didn't anybody want to adopt you?"

"I was adopted three times," Jalen mumbled. "The people kept sending me back. They said I set fire to their homes—but it wasn't true. I didn't do it, Dizil. I *didn't.*"

Three different fires, in three different homes? No way! Jalen had to be lying. I was really interested because Alphs can't lie. (Well, we can, but it makes us vomit purple slime for a week, so we don't.)

"What happened to your parents?" I asked. I wondered whether or not Jalen would tell another lie. He didn't, though. Instead he just glared at me. Then he told me that it was none of my business.

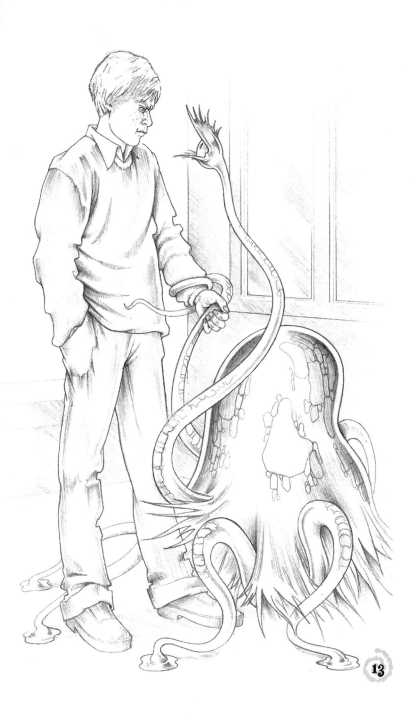

He took a deep breath and looked out of the window. His skin turned even paler, and his two hands started shaking. Suddenly I realized that the Earther kid was scared.

Scared and lonely. Just like me.

So I wrapped my pull-tentacle around his wrist. Then I took him outside to meet the others.

# Chapter 2

# We Meet Dr. Kari

The other aliens were amazed by Jalen. After all, most of us had never had a chance to take a close look at an Earther. They crowded around him. They ruffled his hair and tugged at his arms to see how they moved.

"He's fairly useless, isn't he?" Fflit said to me. "No sparks or anything."

Rasska scratched his nose-horn with his claws. "Earthers are funny-looking things," he agreed. "But maybe he can do something cool with his brain. You know, like your translating stuff, Dizil."

Jalen didn't like standing there while the others talked about him. "I can *think*," he said, glaring around the circle of orphans. "Humans don't need special mind powers because we're smarter than you aliens."

By now I'd guessed that Jalen turned nasty when he was feeling scared. The others didn't know that, though. Rasska's claws curled, and Fflit started sparking. But before a fight could start, Ms. Mack came rushing out. She clapped her hands loudly.

"Children!" she said. "There's a special visitor waiting in the main hall. His name is Dr. Kari. He's one of the top scientists in GalCorp. He's an expert on aliens, and he wants to meet and speak with all of you."

With an excited wave of her hand, Ms. Mack urged us into the hall. Then she said, "Say hello to Dr. Kari, everyone."

Dr. Kari was an Earther, like Jalen. He was pale and bony. He had bright black eyes that seemed to watch everybody at once. He marched onto the stage. Then he began making a long, boring speech about how great the Galactic Corporation was.

"Most of the planets have joined GalCorp. So now we can work together to make a better galaxy," he told us. "And you orphans can help by telling us about your home planets and yourselves. I'm sure that you know many interesting secrets. For example, some of you might know how to use your mind like a weapon to protect yourself."

We all stared at the floor. (We don't like talking about our home planets because we know we may never go home again.) But Dr. Kari didn't seem to notice. He just turned and began marching up and down again. Suddenly he fell straight through a hole in the stage!

Total silence was followed by a sound like music. At first I thought it was an Earth bird singing outside. Then I realized that Jalen was laughing. That set everyone off. Fflit sparked and hissed. Rasska stamped his feet. I hummed through my voice-tentacle. (That's what Alphs do instead of giggling.)

Ms. Mack sucked in her lips to stop herself from laughing along with us. She reached into the hole and pulled out Dr. Kari. He glared at her. Then he brushed clouds of dust from his suit, his hair, and his eyebrows. All of a sudden, he dropped to his knees and ran his finger around the hole.

"Who did this?" he asked, looking up at us. "Please tell me. I promise that you won't get into trouble."

I poked my eye-tentacle into the air and looked down at the hole.

It was a perfect circle, slightly scorched
at the edges. It was as round and neat
as if someone had cut it with a laser saw.
Dr. Kari watched and waited, but no one
spoke.

Finally Ms. Mack shrugged. Then she said, "Fflit burns holes in things sometimes, but we would've seen the sparks. Besides, my orphans would never play a trick like that. Let's go and have a nice cup of tea in my office, Doctor. That'll make you feel better."

She flapped her hands, and all of the kids ran away. Except for me. Dr. Kari was muttering to himself, and I wanted to know what he was saying. So I hung around and sent my ear-tentacle snaking across the floor.

"It's true," the doctor was whispering. "The aliens really *do* have special mind weapons. I must learn the secret of mindfire. Then I'll be the most powerful person in GalCorp. I just need to find out who burned that hole in the floor!"

# Chapter 3

# Dr. Kari
# Takes Over

A week later, Ms. Mack was let go. And suddenly, Dr. Kari became the director of the Home. After that, things started to change. First he called us into his office. He asked hundreds of questions about our home planets. Then he took us to his lab, connected us to weird machines, and did tests.

The other orphans hated the doctor and his tests. As for Jalen and me—well, in a way we were better off than before. It appeared as if Dr. Kari could only speak a few alien languages. So he needed me to translate for him. And he chose Jalen as his assistant because he was an Earther like him.

Jalen loved working with the computers, and we were allowed to wander freely around the place. The others were mostly shut away in their rooms.

At first this all made life harder for Jalen. After he became Dr. Kari's special pet, the other aliens started to bully him. They played mean tricks on him, too. Fflit was the worst. It sparked so much at Jalen that his hands and clothes were dotted with tiny burn marks.

Jalen pretended that he didn't care, but it was an act. I found him in Dr. Kari's lab one day, putting burn cream on his hands. He was muttering, "I'll get Fflit for this."

"Not *more* fighting," I sighed. "Couldn't you just be nice to Fflit instead of being so nasty?"

"No," Jalen said. "Back off, Dizil. I don't need friends. In fact, I don't need anyone at all. I can look after myself."

"Yeah, sure," I said, running my eye-tentacle across his burns. "For such a smart kid, you can be really stupid."

Jalen can't stand being called stupid, so that made him stop and think. The next night, all of us were watching movies after dinner. Jalen pulled out a huge block of chocolate from his pocket. Aliens *love* chocolate, and we all stared at it hungrily. Jalen said, "I found this in Dr. Kari's office, but I don't like sweet things. Does anyone want a piece?"

Like I said, Jalen is smart. The chocolate was great. And it tasted even better because we thought that he'd stolen it from the doctor!

Jalen was still rude to everyone. But now, instead of getting angry, the kids just laughed.

Jalen kept saying that he didn't need friends, but I think we were friends just the same. One night, after Dr. Kari yelled at him for something, Jalen told me about what had happened to his parents. They were killed by mistake when GalCorp guards started shooting at some rebels.

I slid my touch-tentacle around his shoulder and said, "OK, I get it. You don't like Dr. Kari because he works for GalCorp. But you're mad at the rebels, too, aren't you? It doesn't matter that they hate GalCorp as much as you do."

"Exactly," Jalen said, as he pushed me away quickly. "You can't trust anyone, Dizil. Just remember that, and you'll be all right."

# Chapter 4

# Morgan Turns Up

A few days later, we were lined up in the main hall waiting for lunch. Suddenly an Earther girl appeared in the doorway. She was taller than Jalen. She had smooth brown skin, curly brown hair, and warm brown eyes. She looked around the hall, smiling at everyone. When she spotted Jalen, her smile got even wider.

"Hey, another Earther," she said, walking over to join us.

The girl told us that her name was Morgan.

When I asked why she'd been sent to the Home, Morgan said no one wanted to adopt her. She explained that her parents had been rebels. They were caught and shot by GalCorp. Wet stuff started dripping out of her eyes. I patted it with my taste-tentacle. "What's that, Morgan?" I asked.

"Tears," she said, dripping faster. "I'm crying. That's what Earthers do when they're sad."

I'd never seen any more wet stuff in Jalen's eyes, even though he still got sad sometimes. I wanted to ask him about that. But when I turned around, he'd vanished without even waiting for lunch. Morgan looked surprised, but ten seconds later she was busy asking questions. Soon Rasska was teaching her how to say hello in Repton, and Fflit was sparking for her. And I was explaining that Jalen was a little funny about rebels because of his parents.

The aliens all liked Morgan, but for some reason Dr. Kari hated her on sight. He called her Rebel Girl. He made her work in the lab, moving around boxes and heavy machines. As soon as Dr. Kari left us alone, Morgan marched over to the computer where Jalen was working.

"Why did you run away from me at lunchtime?" she asked.

Jalen said, "I didn't."

"Yes, you did," Morgan told him. "I was sad, because I want us to be friends."

It was the worst thing she could've said. Jalen glared. Then he began making his usual speech about how he didn't need anybody. Morgan tugged at one of her curls. Then she said, "OK, so you don't want any friends. What *do* you want?"

"I want power," Jalen said quickly. "I'm too smart to stay in this place. As soon as I get out of here, I'm going to do something big. Then I'll be so powerful that nobody can boss me around ever again."

Morgan frowned and said, "But GalCorp controls everything and bosses around everyone. No one will ever really be free until we all get together and stop them. I thought that you, of all people, would want to stop GalCorp, Jalen. After all, they killed your par . . ."

Before Morgan could finish the rest of her sentence, Jalen jumped up. He glared at me and walked out.

"Oh, no," I groaned as he left. "Me and my big voice-tentacle. I shouldn't have told you about his parents, Morgan. Jalen will be angry at both of us now."

Sure enough, Jalen wouldn't speak to us for days. I felt awful. Besides, I really needed to talk to him about something I'd just learned. Some GalCorp divers had found an alien spaceship at the bottom of the sea.

Since Dr. Kari was GalCorp's expert on aliens, they brought the spaceship to the Home. They parked it right next to the doctor's personal flyer. Dr. Kari checked the ship out and decided that the aliens must have used mindfire to power it. And he was right.

The spaceship was my parents' ship, and my First Father had the power of mindfire. He used it to start the engines. Then my other fathers and mothers would pilot the ship. I didn't trust Dr. Kari, so I didn't want him to know how to use the ship. (Our spaceships are pretty special—they are the best in the galaxy.)

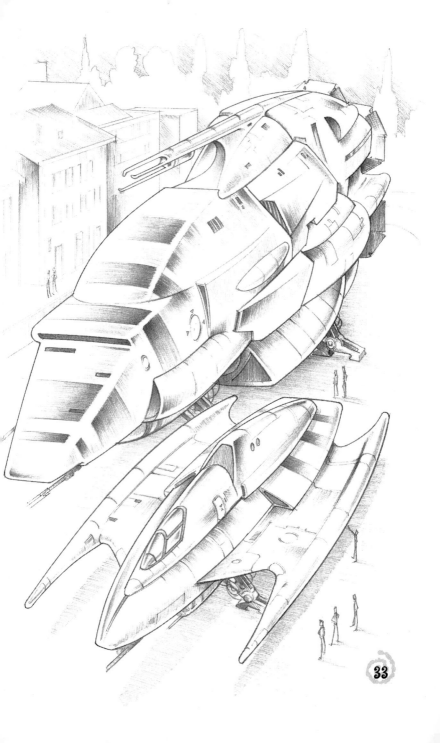

33

I kept hoping that Jalen would help us stop Dr. Kari from learning how the spaceship worked. But he just kept on being rude to the rest of us. In fact, he was so rude that Fflit began to spark at him again.

Jalen gave Fflit a nasty smile. "I could get you for that," he said. "But why bother? You'll be gone by next Friday."

He turned and walked off. Morgan and I went racing after him. "Wait a minute," Morgan gasped. "What do you mean?"

"I meant what I said," Jalen told her. "Now that Dr. Kari has that spaceship, he doesn't need Fflit and the others anymore. He's sending them all to zoos."

Jalen continued, "You and I are safe, Morgan, because we're Earthers. And Dr. Kari is keeping Dizil to help him. I don't care about the others. Why should I? They never cared about me."

Morgan tugged at a handful of curls. "But it's wrong to put the others in zoos. Can't you see that?" Jalen just stared blankly at her. Morgan shrugged and said, "All right then. I'll have to rescue the aliens myself. Maybe I can hack into Dr. Kari's computer and . . ."

"No way!" Jalen said sharply. "You don't know a thing about computers. *I'll* think of a plan, Morgan. Just remember, I'm only doing this to stop you from making a mess of things. I certainly don't care about helping the other orphans!"

# We Get Away

Over the next three days, Morgan and Jalen discussed ways to outsmart Dr. Kari. Between the two of them, they must have come up with a dozen or more plans. And once they settled on one plan, they worked on it nonstop.

Jalen was so excited that he didn't even bother to sleep. He loved the idea of stealing the keys for the doctor's flyer and having everyone get away in it.

And he laughed when he thought about Dr. Kari finding that the orphans and his flyer had vanished.

By Thursday, we were ready to move on the plan. My job was to keep Dr. Kari busy while the others sneaked out to the flyer. I went to his office after lunch. I started asking all sorts of questions about the alien spaceship. (The doctor could talk about the ship for hours.)

I'd been asking Dr. Kari questions for about 20 minutes. Suddenly he narrowed his eyes at me. "That's very interesting, Dizil," he said. "I notice that you have 12 tentacles . . . and there are 12 controls on the pilot seat in the spaceship."

The next minute, he twisted my tentacles into a knot and marched me up to his lab. Then he strapped me into one of the machines. "I want to know everything about that ship," he demanded. "If you don't tell me, I'm going to start this machine. And you won't like what happens then."

I tucked my voice-tentacle under the seat to show that I wasn't going to talk. Dr. Kari laughed and reached for the switch that started the machine. Then he yelped and yanked back his hand. He started blowing on his fingers.

"My hand is burning," he moaned. "Look, it's smoking!"

I lifted my eye-tentacle and peered over his shoulder. There was Jalen, standing in the doorway. Morgan and Rasska were right behind him. As they raced to help me out of the machine, Dr. Kari started backing away quickly.

"Well, well," he said, staring at his hand. "The mindfire. Quite impressive, Jalen. So you had it all along. I suspected that you might have been the one, but I couldn't be sure . . . not until now."

Then he ducked into the hallway. He slammed the door, locking us in. "Oh, no," Rasska muttered. "The flyer will be taking off in ten minutes. We told the others to leave without us if we weren't back in time."

He kicked the door with his big clawed foot. Morgan ran at it. I poked my touch-tentacle into the lock. Nothing worked. We were just about to give up when Jalen pushed past us. He said, "Dr. Kari's a fool. I won't let him beat us. Stand back."

He stared angrily at the door for a second. It burst into flames. Mindfire! It would've been scary, except that we didn't have time to be scared. Rasska kicked the door again, and it fell apart. We jumped over the red-hot coals, ran downstairs, and tumbled into the yard.

We were just in time to watch the flyer lift off the ground and soar into the air.

"The spaceship!" I gasped, racing over to it. "Come on. Hurry!"

The hatch opened when I pressed my touch-tentacle against the locking panel. We piled inside, and I collapsed into the pilot seat. "Okay, Jalen," I shouted. "Aim your mindfire at the engine so that we can start the ship."

Nothing happened. When I looked around, Jalen whispered, "Sorry, Dizil. I can't. I've only used the mindfire by accident when I was angry. I don't know how to make it work on purpose."

I groaned, and Rasska started yelling in Repton. But Morgan walked over to Jalen. She rested her hand on his shoulder. "Now, Jalen, just think about Dr. Kari for a minute or two," she said softly. "Do you want him to beat us?"

I could see that Jalen was listening closely to Morgan's words. I crossed two of my tentacles for luck and held my breath.

Suddenly Jalen snarled, "No!" And as his face went red with anger, the mindfire hit the engine. The spaceship took off.

# More Trouble Ahead

The ship passed Earth's moon and shot out into space. At that point, the four of us sighed and relaxed.

"Well, we've escaped from Dr. Kari and the Home," Jalen said. "And now we have something that makes us *really* powerful—this alien spaceship."

"Yes, this is an awesome spaceship," Morgan agreed. "With a ship like this, we can fight Dr. Kari and GalCorp and win. We can make a difference to everyone in the galaxy. I just know it!"

Jalen glared at Morgan. She glared back at him. Rasska nudged me with his scaly elbow, nearly knocking me off my seat.

"Just look at them," he whispered. "We'd better watch out, Dizil. I think there's more trouble ahead."

# About the Author

*Jenny Pausacker*

Jenny Pausacker has been
a science fiction fan for a very
long time. She has written
22 books and several short stories
for children and young adults.

Jenny is a big fan of *Star Wars,*
and she owns a complete set
of *Star Wars* models.

Photograph by James Spence

# About the Illustrator

*Brian Harrison*

Brian has always loved drawing and had his first solo exhibition when he was 11 years old.

Brian often annoyed his teachers when they would discover his wonderful drawings on desktops and inside schoolbooks. He was surprised that they didn't appreciate his efforts!

Brian has lived and traveled in many parts of the world, including Europe, the Middle East, and Africa. He now lives with his wife, 2 dogs, and 20 goats on a farm.

Brian illustrates children's books and produces artwork for advertising agencies.